P9-DBU-458

A Note to Parents and Caregivers:

Read-it! Readers are for children who are just starting on the amazing road to reading. These beautiful books support both the acquisition of reading skills and the love of books.

The RED LEVEL presents familiar topics using common words and repeating sentence patterns.
The BLUE LEVEL presents new ideas using a larger vocabulary and varied sentence structure.
The YELLOW LEVEL presents more challenging ideas, a broad vocabulary, and wide variety in sentence structure.

When sharing a book with your child, read in short stretches, pausing often to talk about the pictures. Have your child turn the pages and point to the pictures and familiar words. And be sure to reread favorite stories or parts of stories.

There is no right or wrong way to share books with children. Find time to read with your child, and pass on the legacy of literacy.

Adria F. Klein, Ph.D.
Professor Emeritus
California State University
San Bernardino, California

First American edition published in 2003 by
Picture Window Books
5115 Excelsior Boulevard
Suite 232
Minneapolis, MN 55416
1-877-845-8392
www.picturewindowbooks.com

First published in Great Britain by Franklin Watts, 96 Leonard Street, London, EC2A 4XD
Text © Damian Kelleher 2000
Illustration © Georgie Birkett 2000

Printed in the United States of America.

Library of Congress Cataloging-in-Publication Data
Kelleher, Damian.
  Selfish Sophie / written by Damian Kelleher ; illustrated by Georgie Birkett.—1st
American ed.
    p. cm. — (Read-it! readers)
  Summary: Sophie is usually selfish with the things she owns, but when her class goes on a
field trip to the zoo, she learns that sharing can be fun.
  ISBN 1-4048-0069-7
  [1. Sharing—Fiction. 2. Selfishness—Fiction. 3. School field trips—Fiction.] I. Birkett,
Georgie, ill. II. Title. III. Series.
  PZ7.D28123 Se 2003
  [E]—dc21   2002072293

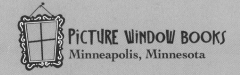

PiCTURE WiNDOW BOOKS
Minneapolis, Minnesota

Selfish Sophie

Written by Damian Kelleher

Illustrated by Georgie Birkett

Reading Advisors:
Adria F. Klein, Ph.D.
Professor Emeritus, California State University
San Bernardino, California

Ruth Thomas
Durham Public Schools
Durham, North Carolina

R. Ernice Bookout
Durham Public Schools
Durham, North Carolina

Picture Window Books
Minneapolis, Minnesota

Sophie wasn't very good
at sharing.

She didn't like to share
her candy.

She didn't like to share
her books.

She didn't like to share her
stuffed animals.

She didn't share any of her
things!

"You know, it's much more fun to share your things," said Sophie's dad.

"They're mine!" said Sophie.

"And no one else can play with them."

13

Sophie's class went on a
trip to the zoo.

Sophie sat all by herself on the bus.

"This is my seat," said Sophie.

Everyone else sat in pairs
and sang songs.

"This is my lunch," said
Sophie.

Everyone else shared their chips and sandwiches.

19

After a while, it started to
rain. It poured and poured.

Everyone got out their umbrellas—

21

everyone except Sophie.

23

Jake was by himself, too.

"Would you like to share my umbrella?" asked Jake.

"Yes, please," said Sophie.

"I'm getting very wet."

On the bus, Sophie and Jake shared a seat.

And they giggled all the way home.

Red Level

The Best Snowman, by Margaret Nash 1-4048-0048-4
Bill's Baggy Pants, by Susan Gates 1-4048-0050-6
Cleo and Leo, by Anne Cassidy 1-4048-0049-2
Felix on the Move, by Maeve Friel 1-4048-0055-7
Jasper and Jess, by Anne Cassidy 1-4048-0061-1
The Lazy Scarecrow, by Jillian Powell 1-4048-0062-X
Little Joe's Big Race, by Andy Blackford 1-4048-0063-8
The Little Star, by Deborah Nash 1-4048-0065-4
The Naughty Puppy, by Jillian Powell 1-4048-0067-0
Selfish Sophie, by Damian Kelleher 1-4048-0069-7

Blue Level

The Bossy Rooster, by Margaret Nash 1-4048-0051-4
Jack's Party, by Ann Bryant 1-4048-0060-3
Little Red Riding Hood, by Maggie Moore 1-4048-0064-6
Recycled!, by Jillian Powell 1-4048-0068-9
The Sassy Monkey, by Anne Cassidy 1-4048-0058-1
The Three Little Pigs, by Maggie Moore 1-4048-0071-9

Yellow Level

Cinderella, by Barrie Wade 1-4048-0052-2
The Crying Princess, by Anne Cassidy 1-4048-0053-0
Eight Enormous Elephants, by Penny Dolan 1-4048-0054-9
Freddie's Fears, by Hilary Robinson 1-4048-0056-5
Goldilocks and the Three Bears, by Barrie Wade 1-4048-0057-3
Mary and the Fairy, by Penny Dolan 1-4048-0066-2
Jack and the Beanstalk, by Maggie Moore 1-4048-0059-X
The Three Billy Goats Gruff, by Barrie Wade 1-4048-0070-0